The Adventures of Jean-Pierre

D0556434

Paul Gallico

The adventures of JEAN-PIERRE

The day the Guinea Pig talked and
The day Jean-Pierre was pignapped

illustrated by Gioia Fiammenghi

A Piccolo book
Pan Books London and Sydney

First published in separate volumes by William Heinemann Ltd
The Day the Guinea Pig Talked first published 1963
© Paul Gallico and Mathemata A.G. 1963
The Day Jean-Pierre Was Pignapped first published 1964
© Paul Gallico and Mathemata A.G. 1964
This Piccolo edition published 1975 by Pan Books Ltd,
Cavaye Place, London SW10 9PG
ISBN 0 330 24358 6

Made and printed in Great Britain by
Richard Clay (The Chaucer Press) Ltd, Bungay, Suffolk

The day the guinea-pig talked

to
**Sarah
More**

In their secret place, down in the cellar in the old stone house, Cecile and Jean-Pierre looked at one another.

Cecile said, 'Jean-Pierre, how I wish you could understand me!'

Jean-Pierre said, 'Oh, Cecile, how I wish you could understand me!'

And both of them said, 'I wish, I wish, I wish you could.'

But they couldn't, for Jean-Pierre was a Guinea Pig. He was a year old and quite clever, but he only spoke Guinea Pig Talk.

Cecile was a little girl. She was eight years old and tall for her age. But Cecile could only speak French, for she *was* French and lived with her father and mother on a farm in the South of France, on a hill behind the city of Cannes.

Jean-Pierre, of course, is French for John-Peter. Cecile had called him that because it seemed a nice name to her. Jean-Pierre liked it. All the other Guinea Pigs he knew had only one name. He had two. He knew that his name was Jean-Pierre and Cecile's name was Cecile. But that was all that he could understand.

Every evening, after Cecile fed him in their secret place in the cellar, she would talk to him in French and he would speak to her in Guinea Pig Talk, and after a while they would just look at one another and wish that they could understand.

For Jean-Pierre had so much to say to Cecile.

And Cecile had so many, many things she wanted to tell Jean-Pierre.

Each was most curious about what the other was thinking.

There seemed to be no way for them ever to find out.

On the farm where Cecile lived was a dog named

Bobi, and a cat named Coco and a rabbit named Gris–Gris. Bobi was rather a long yellow dog with a long, yellow tail but he had a nice smile. Coco was black with three white feet. Gris-Gris was grey and cuddly but very stupid.

Cecile was fond of them but most of all she cared

about Jean-Pierre, because he was her very own. Bobi belonged to her in a way and so did Coco and Gris-Gris, but Jean-Pierre belonged to her most of all because she had bought him with her own pocket-money from a pet shop in Cannes. He cost five francs. She had been saving up this money to buy a skipping-rope.

Five francs in French money is the same thing as seven shillings. Seven shillings is not much if you have hundreds of billions of shillings or even millions, but if seven shillings are the only shillings you have and you need them to buy a skipping-rope, it is the most money in the world.

Cecile went to school in Cannes which was five miles from the farm. Her mother took her there every morning on the bus and called for her every afternoon.

From the bus stop it was only a short walk to the school and on the way they had to pass the pet shop.

They passed it going in the morning and they passed it coming back in the afternoon.

One day, Cecile saw Jean-Pierre in the window in a cage with eight other Guinea Pigs. The cage was on a shelf, just high enough to let Cecile look into the faces of the Guinea Pigs when she passed. And of course, if they wanted to, the Guinea Pigs could look into hers.

The other eight Guinea Pigs took no notice at all when Cecile went past. They went on munching their lettuce leaves, or sleeping in little heaps in a corner, so that you could not tell where one began and the other left off.

But Jean-Pierre (though at that time he was not

known as Jean-Pierre, since he did not yet belong to
anyone and had no name) always looked up at Cecile in
the strangest way.

It was the kind of look which meant there was something on the tip of his tongue he wanted to say to her.

He was different from the other Guinea Pigs because
he came all the way from Abyssinia. Abyssinia is in
Africa. His fur was long and rough instead of short and
smooth like ordinary Guinea Pigs. His colour was
rather like a frying-pan which had been left out in the
rain and had gone rusty. Thus, while he was mostly
black, it was not a real proper black but more of a
browny-black. Only his ears were much lighter and so

fine you could almost see right through them. His nose was pink and so were his feet. His whiskers were white and very clean, because he kept them that way. But his eyes were golden.

The eyes of all the other Guinea Pigs were either black like beads, or brown like coffee beans. Only the eyes of Jean-Pierre were golden, and his fur rough instead of smooth.

Cecile saw at once that Jean-Pierre was a very special Guinea Pig.

Jean-Pierre noticed Cecile the very first time she went by the window, after their cage had been put there. But, of course, then he did not know that her name was Cecile.

He only knew he liked her.

She was not as pretty as some of the other little girls who went past the window, but it didn't matter. Her hair was so browny brown that it was almost black. Her skin was brown too, from the sun. Her nose turned up a little and was covered with freckles. Her teeth were white and even, but two of them in front were missing, as is usual with little girls that age. Only her eyes were not like those of anyone else he had ever seen. They were neither blue nor brown nor even green. They were grey.

And the very first time that she stopped to look into the window as she passed, it seemed to Jean-Pierre as though there was something on the tip of her tongue she wanted to say to him too. He wondered what it was.

Thereafter, every morning and every afternoon, each

time Cecile and her mother went by, Cecile would stop to look at Jean-Pierre.

And Jean-Pierre would also pause at whatever he was doing, which might be gnawing at the core of an apple, or tidying up his fur, or even scratching himself. Then he would come over to the window and look at Cecile.

Later, at home, when she was not busy with her lessons, but mostly at night when she was alone in bed, she thought about Jean-Pierre. For by this time, that was the name she had given him.

She wondered why his eyes were golden. She wondered why he was so special and different.

She could hardly wait for each new morning when she would pass the shop where she would be able to see him again.

Jean-Pierre was feeling exactly the same.

When he was not busy eating, or tidying his fur and whiskers, but mostly at night when he joined a heap of his friends in the corner, and just before he went to sleep, he thought about the little girl with the brown face.

He wondered why her eyes were grey and so very clear, not like the eyes of other people. He wondered why she was so special.

He could hardly wait for each new morning when she would pass the shop and he could see her again.

One day, Cecile's mother asked her, 'Must you stop every time we go past here? What is it you are staring at?' For the window of the pet shop was full of all kinds of other little animals as well as Guinea Pigs.

There were puppies and kittens and turtles and goldfish and canaries, a parrot and even a monkey.

Cecile had replied, 'Can't you see? It's Jean-Pierre,' and she pointed to him as he came over to the window and looked at her.

Cecile's mother smiled, 'How do you know he is called Jean-Pierre?' she asked.

'Because that is what I have named him,' Cecile replied.

Sometime later Cecile had a terrible fright.

When she passed the window of the shop, she saw there were only seven Guinea Pigs, where before there had always been nine. Someone had bought two.

Cecile cried, 'Oh, Mummy,' (in French, of course) and caught at her mother's arm. 'What if one of them were to be Jean-Pierre?'

Luckily, Jean-Pierre was still there and he came over at once to see her.

And while it did not show, Jean-Pierre was feeling very pale and frightened himself.

A hand had reached into the cage and taken out two of his friends, and they never came back. From then on, whenever anyone came into the shop, Jean-Pierre hid beneath the heap of the other Guinea Pigs.

But Cecile decided that day that she must buy Jean-Pierre.

When her mother learned this, she said, 'Oh dear, Cecile. Haven't we enough pets already without another? We have Bobi and Coco and Gris-Gris.'

'But they aren't really mine,' Cecile cried. 'They just

live with us.' Because, of course, every farm has a dog and a cat and at least one rabbit.

Cecile's mother said, 'You will have to pay for him yourself then, out of your own pocket-money. Do you really want him that badly?'

Cecile did not reply, but only nodded her head to say yes. She could not tell her mother why it was she wanted Jean-Pierre so much. During all the days she had been passing by and stopping to look at him, and he at her, something secret had grown up between them. Something shared. Something that made them feel that they belonged to one another. But neither knew what it was, only that they wanted to be together.

That day at school, Cecile's teacher had to speak to her twice for not paying attention.

Indeed, it was only too true. Cecile was not listening. She was thinking about Jean-Pierre and whether she had enough money in her little wooden box at home to pay for him. For she had no idea how much a Guinea Pig might cost.

That evening, when she got home, she took all of the pocket-money she had saved up, out of the little wooden box. She counted it three times, and then once more, just in *case* she had made a mistake, and then tied it up in her handkerchief, for she had no purse.

At last, next afternoon when they came from school, Cecile and her mother went into the pet shop to inquire the price of the Guinea Pig.

The woman in charge of the shop told them, most politely, that the Guinea Pigs were five francs each.

Her mother asked Cecile, 'Have you five francs?'

Cecile gave a great sigh of relief. She had been so frightened the woman might have said ten francs, or fifty francs or even one hundred francs. For how could one tell what a very special Guinea Pig like Jean-Pierre might cost?

But five francs, or seven shillings, was exactly what Cecile had. For she had been saving up for a skipping-rope which cost six francs. It cost that much because it was a very special skipping-rope, an English one, which would have enabled her to skip better and faster than anyone else in school.

It is a strange thing to do, when you have been saving up to buy something like a special skipping-rope, to change your mind and buy a very special Guinea Pig instead. But Cecile could not help herself.

For Jean-Pierre had come over and was looking at her out of his golden eyes, as though saying to her, 'Oh, please buy me.'

Which, indeed, *was* exactly what he was saying to her, only not in so many words.

Then, as they stood there looking at one another for a moment, again that strange, secret feeling was shared between them. If only they might understand one another.

Cecile was quite sure then that it was better to have a very special Guinea Pig, rather than a very special, English skipping-rope.

'Five francs each,' the woman repeated, 'and the little girl can choose whichever one she likes.'

Cecile reached into her pocket, took out her handkerchief in which the money was tied, and paid the five francs.

'Now, which one do you want?' the woman asked Cecile.

Cecile did not even have to point. Jean-Pierre was already waiting at the door of the cage, for he was a clever little Guinea Pig. And there was something about the way he sat there looking so eagerly at Cecile, and waiting for her to open the door, that showed he was now a most happy, as well as clever and special, Guinea Pig.

The woman who owned the shop smiled and said to Cecile's mother, 'Why, he acts as though he knows your little girl already.'

Cecile thought to herself a private thought, which

was never spoken aloud, because it would not have been polite to have done so. It was: *How very stupid grown-up people can be. They just don't ever know anything!* Of course she and Jean-Pierre knew each other.

She opened the door of his cage and took him into her hand, he was fat, soft, warm, and his little heart seemed to be beating a thousand to the minute with joy and excitement. Cecile held him to her cheek for a moment and then looked into his golden eyes, which were filled with all the things he seemed to be wanting to say to her. But she knew she would have to take him away and to a secret place, where they could be alone, before she would ever be able to find out what it was.

The farm on which Cecile lived with her father and mother was a different kind of farm from any you might have ever known or seen. Cecile's father did not grow wheat, or corn, or oats or hay. Nor did he raise pigs, or sheep, or cows like other farmers. Instead he grew thousands and thousands of carnations of every colour and kind, and thousands upon thousands of roses as well. He also grew geraniums, cyclamen, anemones, gladioli and tiger lilies. It was a flower farm.

True, there was an apple orchard behind the old stone house, and some pear and plum trees, and a long grape arbour leading up to the door of the house. In the autumn, when the grapes were full and heavy and purple, the grape arbour was like a tunnel.

They kept a few chickens on the farm for fresh eggs. There were also some pigeons flying about. And, of course, there was Bobi and Coco and Gris-Gris. But all the rest was flowers.

Instead of fields there were rows and rows of terraces, like huge steps going downhill from the house. Here the flowers grew, some in the open, some under cover. They began their life snug in glasshouses, in small pots as seedlings, until two tiny green leaves showed above the black earth. Then they were moved to bigger pots and bigger glasshouses, until they were old enough to live outdoors. That was what a flower farm was like.

From the window of her bedroom Cecile looked out on to the rows and rows of flowers. And in the distance was the Mediterranean Sea.

A sea is almost the same as an ocean, though not quite as large. It was blue and sparkling when the sun shone. When there was a storm it was grey and angry.

Life on a flower farm upon a hillside looking down upon a blue sea is wonderful. One can not only smell the flowers but also see them in all their beautiful colours. There were pink roses, white and red carnations, salmon-coloured geraniums, orange tiger-lilies and lavender cyclamen.

This was where Jean-Pierre came to live with Cecile.

During the day when Cecile was at school, Jean-Pierre's wooden cage stood in the window of the barn where he could look out across the courtyard, past the well and the little house where the pigeons lived, to the woods on the hill where the pine trees waved their arms and nodded their green heads.

The wind would bring the scent of the flowers to Jean-Pierre. He would sit with his pink nose to the bars of the cage, smelling them. They made his nose twitch. After his nose twitched for a while he would sneeze. He liked sneezing.

But when Cecile came home from school, or on Sundays after she was bathed and dressed, she would go and fetch him and take him to their secret place.

It was down in the cellar of the old stone farmhouse. It was not really and truly secret since everybody knew where it was. But Cecile's mother and father did not often go there and so it was secret enough for Cecile and Jean-Pierre.

One of the reasons that Cecile took Jean-Pierre down there was so that they could be alone together.

For grown-ups would never understand that she and her Guinea Pig had most important things to say to one another. And that someday they even hoped to be able to understand WHAT they were saying.

Some people think that Guinea Pigs do not make any kind of noise. Cecile knew that this was not true. For from the very first moment she had him, Jean-Pierre had been full of sounds.

When she held him close to her ear she could hear him grunt softly almost like a little pig. Well, of course he *was* a Guinea Pig.

Sometimes he would squeal. Or click his teeth

together. He could chirrup like a sparrow or croak like a frog. And when he was alarmed he would even give a small shriek.

But all of this was Guinea Pig Talk and Cecile could not understand a word of it. Cecile's dearest wish was that she might understand what he was saying to her. Sometimes she pretended she did, when she put her ear close to his pink nose and listened to his tiny noises. But she knew it was pretend all the time.

It was the same for Jean-Pierre. For him, Cecile made all kinds of noises too, whispers, shouts and cries, some of which hurt his tender little ears. And at no time could he understand a single thing she was saying. For, of course, it was all human talk and French as well.

Another reason for taking Jean-Pierre down to the secret place was that Cecile fed him there. There was a kind of stone shelf in the cellar, not far from a small electric light globe all covered with dust and cobwebs. It was dark enough to be properly secret, yet light enough to see.

This shelf was most useful in more ways than one. It did not matter if Jean-Pierre made a mess on it, and he usually did when he had his dinner. It was easy to clean, but best of all it was just the right height. When Cecile stood up straight she could rest her chin upon it. Then she and Jean-Pierre could look into one another's faces as they used to do when Cecile passed the pet shop on her way to and from school.

This was important, for when Cecile had to look down upon Jean-Pierre all she could see was his browny back with its black marking somewhat in the shape of a potato.

And when Jean-Pierre had to look up at Cecile, all *he* could see were her legs going up past her knees and into her skirts like two thin tree-trunks.

But when Cecile put Jean-Pierre on the stone shelf in the cellar it was just right. In this way they could look at one another face to face for as long as they liked.

Jean-Pierre's dinner was made up of all kinds of things, some of which Cecile brought down from the kitchen, such as lettuce or cabbage leaf, crumbs of bread or cake and a bit of cheese, and others which were stored in the cellar. These were treats like slices of pumpkin, apples, pears, grapes, or pieces of pomegranate.

Perhaps best of all Jean-Pierre loved pomegranate.

A pomegranate is a fruit which grows in the south of France and other warm countries. It looks like a large red apple and has a hard skin almost like a shell. It is full of small red seeds bursting with sweet juice. The seeds were not only good to eat, but also fun. For when Jean-Pierre bit into them the juice got all over his whiskers and face and then Cecile would have to wipe them with her handkerchief.

While Cecile was busy setting out his dinner, Jean-Pierre would sit up on his hind legs like a squirrel and sniff. His golden eyes rolled from one side to the other as he tried to see what he was going to have. But, of course, the most excitement was when Cecile gave him a piece of pomegranate, which she would save for last.

Cecile would rest her chin upon the edge of the stone shelf and watch him while he ate. Jean-Pierre was a little greedy and never finished what he started. He would have a bit of lettuce leaf, then gnaw upon an apple core, have a taste of pumpkin, suck a grape, nibble at a carrot, push his little face right inside a ripe fig, eat some pear or a mouthful of stale cheese, or perhaps go the other way round. At the end he ate the pomegranate. He would take out a red seed, hold it between his paws, bite into it and drink the juice, while making tiny noises of delight.

And when at last he had finished, he would come over to Cecile to have his nose wiped. Then he would comb his whiskers with his paws and tidy up his fur.

After that they would both look at one another

silently for a long time. Both were filled with the wonder of what they saw.

For a Guinea Pig is a most perfect thing, especially one like Jean-Pierre, whose nose was exactly the right colour of pink, not too dark and not too light. Every one of his whiskers was just the right distance from the other, not too long and not too short. His fur was soft and shiny, every hair in place. And his little feet had the loveliest of tiny toenails. Most beautiful of all were his golden eyes, which were like a still pool reflecting a golden sunset. Cecile felt if only somehow she could get to the bottom of this pool, she would find there and understand all the things Jean-Pierre seemed to be trying to say to her.

And a little girl too, is a most perfect thing, especially one like Cecile. For her dark hair was as fine and smooth as silk, her mouth as red as pomegranate seeds and her face was as brown as an autumn leaf.

Most wonderful were her eyes, and Jean-Pierre felt that behind them lay all the things which Cecile seemed to be trying to say to him and which he could not understand.

'Oh, Jean-Pierre,' Cecile would sigh, 'why can't you talk to me?'

But in Jean-Pierre's tiny ears it only sounded like the passing of the wind through the trees.

'Oh, Cecile,' Jean-Pierre cried, 'why can't you talk to me?'

But to Cecile it only sounded like a far-off twitter.

It wasn't at all that way with Bobi, the yellow dog,

and Coco, the black cat. Cecile knew what they were thinking all the time. She knew when Bobi wanted to go out and when he wanted to come in. It was almost like talking. He had one kind of a bark when he had something up a tree, and another when he had something down a hole. He had a 'Let's-go-for-a-walk' bark and a 'Here-comes-a-stranger' bark. He could also say 'Isn't it a lovely day?' just by the way he waved his long, yellow tail.

It was the same with Coco. You could tell when she was pleased and you knew when she was angry. It was plain when she wanted to be loved and when she wanted to be alone. She never actually *said* anything, but she never left anyone in doubt that she did not want people to sit on the chair on which she liked to sleep. She also did not like water, or a cold wind, or smelly people, or to be disturbed when she was watching a mouse-hole.

Cecile somehow had never found herself wishing that she could talk to Bobi, or wondering what Coco was thinking as she lay with her feet tucked up under her. And she certainly had never thought of wanting to have a word with Gris-Gris, the rabbit.

With Jean-Pierre it was different. From the very first time she had laid eyes on him, she wanted to know what he was thinking, as he looked up so eagerly into her face. And now that he was her very own and they could be together, she felt it a hundred times more strongly. Whenever she carried him about, she held his little warm body close to her cheek, to listen to the soft sounds he was making, hoping sometime she would understand.

For it would be the most wonderful thing in the world to have a Guinea Pig to whom one could *tell* things, secrets and the like, sad things and happy things that one could not say to grown-ups or even one's school-friends.

And then Jean-Pierre, at the same time, could tell her all he knew. Sometimes he looked to be so full of words to say, that it seemed as though his sides would burst. They would be things that no little girl had ever heard before.

Once, Cecile's mother asked her, 'What on earth do you do down there in the cellar for hours with Jean-Pierre?'

Cecile replied, 'Nothing.' And then added, 'Oh, I wish, I wish, I wish Jean-Pierre could speak to me! Today he *almost* did.'

Cecile's mother said, 'Oh, darling, you know very well that animals can't speak.'

Cecile did not mind her mother saying this. It was just like all grown-ups who didn't understand. It only made her wish the harder.

Since it never ever came any closer than 'almost', Cecile kept on wishing. The longer they were friends, the harder she wished.

She even took to adding her wish, silently, to the end of her prayers at night. When she was all finished with those she asked God to bless (and after Mummy and Daddy came a long list of grandmothers, aunts, uncles, cousins and friends), and before she said her Amen, she would quickly think to herself, *Oh, and please let Jean-Pierre talk to me.*

In the dark, in the corner of his cage on his little bed of straw, Jean-Pierre was doing the very same thing every night when he said his prayers. It took him longer to get to it because he had so many more of everyone than Cecile. He had brothers, sisters, aunts and uncles by the dozens, cousins by the hundreds and more grandparents than anyone could imagine. But when he had reached the end of the list, he would add, '*And, oh please let Cecile talk to me.*'

And so the days passed.

One Sunday morning, which ought not to have been different from any other morning, Cecile woke up, sat up in bed and felt very odd. She felt special.

She felt most special.

That very same Sunday morning, and at the very same time, Jean-Pierre woke up in his little nest of straw. He lifted his pink nose from beneath his pink paws. He sniffed. He sneezed. And HE felt special.

He, too, felt *most* special.

Looking out of her window, Cecile saw the sun and the sea. The blue Mediterranean was shining as though it were covered with gold and diamonds. The sun had

not yet climbed high into the sky. It seemed to be resting for a moment upon the edge of the water, so close, it seemed to Cecile as though they were talking to one another.

She had never seen anything like this before. And the first thought that came to her was, *Could this perhaps be the day that Jean-Pierre and I will be able to speak to one another?*

Each new morning she hoped that it might be, but this was the first morning ever when she felt as though it could really happen.

Jean-Pierre looked out of the window to the trees on

the hillside. They were rustling and nodding and their branches were touching one another, as though they were holding hands and whispering together.

Jean-Pierre had never noticed this before, and he thought, *Could this be the day, perhaps, when Cecile and I will be able to speak to one another?*

When Cecile got out of her bed she had a tingling all over and a peculiar feeling in her tummy.

Can you remember what it is like when you wake up in the morning and know that it is your birthday? Or Christmas? Or that at last the day has arrived when you will be going off on holiday to the seaside? That was how Cecile felt.

It wasn't her birthday. It wasn't Christmas. She wasn't going anywhere at all. But she was filled with excitement. She felt that if she gave a leap she would fly right out through the window. She did not do so because she had more sense. But the tingling all over and the feeling in her tummy told her that something tremendous might be going to happen that day.

Exactly the same thing was happening to Jean-Pierre, except that being a Guinea Pig he felt it in different places.

With him it began with a kind of tickling in his nose. The tickling then ran between his ears and along his back, right down to the place where his tail ought to have been, if he had had one. Guinea Pigs, however, have no tails.

Then he sneezed four times and felt that if he gave a leap he could fly through the bars of his cage, out of the window, past the pump in the courtyard, over the roofs of the glasshouses and right to the top of the trees.

He didn't do so because he had more sense. But the tickling which had now spread all over him, even to his pink toes, and three more sneezes, told him also that something tremendous might be going to happen to him that day.

The water that morning in Cecile's bath looked like silver, and when it ran from the tap it sang a little song to her. The soap kept out of her eyes. She was dry in a jiffy. Her clothes seemed fairly to leap on to her back. Other times, Cecile was rather slow in dressing. It was that kind of day!

As Jean-Pierre set about giving his fur its morning clean, the sun crept through the door of the barn and across the floor, like a river of gold. Other times it took Jean-Pierre quite a while to comb the tangles out of his fur, put his whiskers right and clear the cobwebs from his eyes. Now everything went quickly. His coat was brushed as smooth as silk. His whiskers straightened. His eyes cleared. And before he knew it he was ready. That was the kind of day it was!

The day was all shivery with excitement, when everything seemed to be different to Cecile. Breakfast tasted better. The eggs were yellower. The toast crisper. The milk was sweeter.

Outside the house even the air seemed softer. The colours of all the flowers in the glasshouses were brighter, and the flowers themselves seemed to know something was going to happen, for when Cecile looked in through the door at them they put their heads together as though they were whispering.

Sounds were not the same either. The church bells rang more joyously. The whistle of the train rushing past down by the sea seemed to say 'Farewell' more sadly. The birds in the woods sounded different. So did the cooing of the pigeons and the sighing of the wind.

As soon as Cecile had finished her breakfast, she ran to get Jean-Pierre and her feet hardly seemed to touch the ground. For whatever it was that would happen, she and Jean-Pierre must be together.

When she went into the barn and opened the door of his cage, he was waiting for her, and she saw at once how special he was, like everything else that special day.

For if his nose had been pink before, it was now twice as pink. And if his whiskers had been white before, they were twice as white now. And his coat shone and his golden eyes were as bright as though little fires burned within them.

Cecile took him in her hand and held him to her face. She whispered, 'Oh, Jean-Pierre. I feel as though something wonderful is going to happen to us today.'

Jean-Pierre did not understand a word, but he thought he almost did.

When he was close to her cheek he whispered in her ear, 'Oh, Cecile. I think something wonderful might be going to happen to us today.'

But it was still Guinea Pig Talk and Cecile didn't understand a word he said. But she thought she almost did.

So it must be going to take place soon.

Then they went out together to look for the place where it would be going to happen to them, whatever it was. Neither Cecile nor Jean-Pierre knew where to look, or what it was going to be, or how they would know.

They went down to the brook and waited. It sang happily as it tumbled downhill over the rocks. But nothing happened there.

They went up into the glen on the hill behind the glasshouses, where the pine trees rustled. They saw a grasshopper fiddling with its legs. But that was all. It didn't happen there.

They went off into the apple orchard and listened to the humming of the bees. An apple fell from a tree with a thud, and Bobi came rushing up and barked at it. But nothing else happened.

They passed beneath the grape arbour, slowly, with Cecile taking care not to step on the cracks of the stones of the walk, just in case. But it made no difference.

They went through the barn into the potting-shed and from there into the hothouse where the tiny seedlings of new flowers were just pushing green leaves above the dark earth in the boxes. They waited. The seedlings seemed to be full of joy to be above the earth at last, but that was all. It didn't happen there either.

They visited the different flowers, on the terraces out of doors, thinking perhaps that they might know the secret. But although before they had seemed to be

whispering to one another, now they only turned silent and watchful.

Yet all through that strange morning, both Jean-Pierre and Cecile *knew* that this was the day for which they had both been longing, and that it must happen somewhere.

They went up into the attic, where Cecile was almost certain it would have to be, because there were so many exciting things there. There were boxes and old news-papers, a chair with only three legs, a table slit down the middle, a spider who let himself down from the roof, and some broken toys with which Cecile didn't play any longer. They found a pair of shoes and an old

hat and all sorts of other things no longer useful. It was dark, with only tiny bits of light shining through the cracks in the red tiles of the roof.

Cecile whispered, 'Shhh, Jean-Pierre. Don't make a sound,' and held his little warm body closer to her face. But after a while it was clear that it was not to be there either. All that took place was that the spider pulled himself up on his silken rope and went back into his hole under the roof.

They came downstairs again, into the hall, not knowing where to go now, for they had been to almost every place.

And then it happened!

Whoever would have thought that the secret was hidden within the old grandfather clock in the hall?

*　　*　　*

The clock was almost as old as the house, which was very old indeed. It was so tall it reached almost to the ceiling. Its face was large and round. Cecile always thought it was rather like a real face. It had a picture of the sun and the moon on it, which were like two eyes. In the middle were two holes into which you put the key to wind the clock and the striker. They were like a nose. And at the bottom there was a place which told you what day of the month it was, and this was like a little mouth. Whenever Cecile passed through the hall, she always felt as though the old clock was watching her.

Its tick was loud and clear. Its tock was even louder

and clearer. But what was really loudest and clearest was when it struck the hour.

This was indeed a great effort. The clock was so old that it took a long time to get ready to strike. First it shook. Then it shivered. Then it buzzed. Then it whirred. Then it made a noise exactly like someone falling downstairs. And then at last it struck. 'Bong! Bong! Bong!'

Its voice was deep and could be heard all over the house and even down in the cellar.

When Cecile passed by that day, with Jean-Pierre still cuddled to her face, she felt as always that the clock was following her with its eyes. This time she stopped and turned around quickly to try to catch it.

And catch it she did.

The clock was watching her. But this time it was not only watching her, it was smiling at her. And not only was it smiling at her, but it seemed to be holding out its hands as though wishing she and Jean-Pierre would come closer.

Cecile went over to the clock, holding Jean-Pierre tightly. She stood on her tiptoes and looked up into its face so that if it did speak to her she would not miss a word.

First the clock said only, as all clocks do, 'Tick-tock, tick-tock.'

But then it changed and said, 'Tock-tick, tock-tick,' as clocks sometimes will if you start counting with the tock instead of with the tick.

And then, to their surprise, it said loud and clear:

'Tick-tock, tick-tock,
 Speak to each other between twelve o'clock.
 Tock-tick, tock-tick,
 Between twelve o'clock,
 You must be quick!'

It was happening at last. Cecile had understood every
word that the clock had said.

And, cuddled in her hand, Jean-Pierre had also
understood, just as though it had been speaking in
Guinea Pig Talk.

At last the thing for which each had wished so hard
was going to happen.

But what did the clock mean by *between* twelve
o'clock? How could something be *between* twelve
o'clock? It was either twelve o'clock or it wasn't. It
could be before twelve or after twelve, but neither
Cecile nor Jean-Pierre had ever heard of such a thing
as between twelve. How naughty of the clock to grant
them their wish and then speak in riddles. They said the
rhyme over to themselves and tried very hard to think
what the clock had meant. . .

'Tick-tock, tick-tock,
 Speak to each other between twelve o'clock.
 Tock-tick, tock-tick,
 Between twelve o'clock,
 You must be quick!'

They simply could not guess, and both looked up

anxiously at the clock to see if perhaps it might have something more to say to them.

But it was silent for the moment and hid its face behind its hands, because it was about to strike the hour of eleven.

And, as you have heard, striking was a most serious matter for the grandfather clock, because everything inside it was so very old.

First it shook. Then it shivered. Then it buzzed. Then it whirred. Then came the noise like someone falling downstairs, and after that it began to strike.

'Bong! Bong! Bong!'

Cecile and Jean-Pierre counted, 'One. Two. Three.'

'Bong! Bong!'

'Four. Five.'

All of a sudden, Cecile gave a loud shriek, and at the same time Jean-Pierre gave a tiny shriek. For each, at the same moment, knew what the clock had been trying to tell them.

Between twelve o'clock must be the time between the first stroke and the last stroke of midday.

Count slowly! One—two—three—four—five—six —seven—eight—nine—ten—eleven—twelve.

They were to be allowed to speak to one another for no more than it would take you to count from one to twelve. That was why the clock had said, 'Be quick!'

Oh, dear! And at the same time, Oh, joy! How wonderful to be the only little girl and the only little Guinea Pig in the whole world to be allowed to talk to one another. But what would they say, or could they

say, or did they want to say during the time the clock
was striking twelve? Especially after they had been
wanting to for so long, and had been saving up for
hours and days and weeks and even a month?

It would have to be something most important. Or
most secret. Or most exciting. Something each would
never be able to forget.

It was now past eleven.

Each tick and each tock was bringing them closer to the magic moment that had been promised.

With a last look back at the grandfather clock, to make sure it had nothing more to tell them, Cecile hurried out of the hall and down the steps to the secret place in the cellar. It was just under the clock on the floor above, where they would be able to hear it strike, and that was where she wanted them to be. But, alas, there was not a great deal of time left to think of what to say.

Cecile thought, *Ought I to tell Jean-Pierre when my birthday is?*

Jean-Pierre thought, *Should I tell Cecile about the day I fell off the shelf in the pet shop and hurt my nose?*

Cecile wondered, *Should I tell Jean-Pierre I was first in school last week?*

Jean-Pierre questioned, *Ought I speak to Cecile about my father winning a Blue Ribbon at a Guinea Pig Show?*

Cecile asked herself, *Would Jean-Pierre like to hear about my cousin Robert, who lives in Paris, coming to stay with us at Christmas?*

Jean-Pierre worried, *Shall I tell Cecile that I am sometimes a little frightened of Coco?*

There were so many things they had to tell one another. Jean-Pierre could count up to ten, before he had to start all over again, but there were many more things than that. And Cecile could count up to a thousand, because she was very good at counting, and there were more things than *that*.

What would YOU say to your Guinea Pig, or your

dog, or your cat, or even your turtle or your goldfish, or your mouse, if you had no more than the time of counting slowly from one to twelve in which to say it?

And what would you like to have them tell *you*, if that was all the time they had to say it?

Down in the cellar Cecile put Jean-Pierre on his stone shelf. She cried, 'Soon, soon, Jean-Pierre! But what am I going to say to you? What *is it* you would like to know?'

And Jean-Pierre sat up and squeaked, 'Oh, Cecile, I have so many, many things to say to you. What is it YOU would most like to hear?'

But they could not understand one another – YET!

On Sundays, as a special treat, Jean-Pierre had his dinner at midday, just like the family. And now Cecile set about getting it for him. But she was so excited over what was going to happen that she hardly knew what she was doing, and became most mixed up.

She was so excited that instead of pumpkin slices, she gave him a banana. Instead of an apple, she gave him a turnip. Instead of pomegranate seeds, she fetched him a dog biscuit, kept in a sack for Bobi. She meant to feed him with some cabbage leaf and instead gave him a plate of sardines, put to one side for Coco the cat. And in place of his usual saucer of milk she poured out some red wine from an old bottle nearby in the cellar.

But Jean-Pierre did not mind. He didn't even notice. Actually, he wasn't hungry. He was too busy trying to decide what to say.

Usually, when Cecile was getting Jean-Pierre his

dinner he would be sitting up on his hind legs, sniffing. This time he was lying flat on his tummy on the stone shelf with his eyes shut and his little pink paws over them, thinking.

Should he tell Cecile about an all-white cousin of his who had pink eyes? Ought he to let her know that sometimes when the window of the barn was left open, and the wind blew down from the north, he was cold? Or would she prefer to hear about an uncle of his who had almost gone to America once?

Cecile didn't even see whether Jean-Pierre was eating his meal, because she was always having to run upstairs and look at the hands on the face of the grandfather clock, to see how near they were to twelve.

And the nearer they came, the harder she tried to find what to say to Jean-Pierre.

Ought she to tell him about the time she had cut her finger on a broken flower-pot, and the doctor had come and put in two stitches, and she hadn't cried? Would he care to hear about the day she had swum one hundred yards and won a diploma which was framed, and hung over her bed? Or would he prefer to know that when she grew up, Cecile was going to be either a nurse, or a teacher, or an artist, or a film star – she had not quite made up her mind which?

Cecile came rushing down the cellar steps. She was out of breath and almost in tears.

'Oh, Jean-Pierre,' she cried, 'it's only two minutes more to twelve and I still don't know what it is I want to tell you.'

Jean-Pierre didn't need to understand Cecile's words. He always knew what time it was by the feeling in the ends of his whiskers. He knew very well that there were only two minutes left to twelve, and he also knew that he had been unable to make up his mind what to tell Cecile when the time came.

Jean-Pierre took his paws from over his face, and opening his golden eyes he looked into the grey ones of Cecile. He saw the tears there. If Guinea Pigs could cry, he too would have done so.

And now, upstairs, through the floor, they heard the grandfather clock shake. Then it shivered. Then it buzzed. Then it whirred. Finally it made the noise like someone falling downstairs and then at last, they heard the deep, booming strike of the hour.

'Bong!' It was the first note of the magic moment between twelve.

And then, suddenly, Cecile didn't have to think any more of what it was she wanted to say. She knew!

She looked into the little browny face, with the pink nose, the white whiskers and the tiny ears, so fine you could almost see through them. She saw a poor little Guinea Pig, with a marking somewhat in the shape of a potato on his back, who wasn't really very pretty. But he was her very own.

And she cried, 'Oh, Jean-Pierre! I love you!'

Jean-Pierre looked into the brown face of Cecile.

Two shining tears still clung to the grey eyes and he no longer had to think what it was he wished to say to her. He also knew.

He saw a lonely little girl, who was really not all *that* pretty, for she had freckles and her nose turned up a little and her hair wasn't too tidy, but she was his very own and they belonged to one another.

'Oh, Cecile!' he cried, 'I love you!'

And then each repeated to one another, 'I love you!'

That was all they said, while upstairs the grandfather clock boomed away the last strokes.

Each had understood. Each had warmed the heart of the other. For the words were the most beautiful ones that a little girl could say to a tiny Guinea Pig. And the words were quite the most beautiful ones that a tiny Guinea Pig could say to a little girl.

In fact they were the most beautiful words that anyone could ever speak to anyone, anywhere, anytime. They were words that anyone could understand, no matter in what language they were spoken.

Cecile picked up Jean-Pierre and, cuddling him under her chin, went upstairs into the hall to say 'thank you' to the grandfather clock.

Cecile stood once more on tiptoes and held Jean-Pierre up to where the clock could see him with the sun and the moon of its eyes, and whispered, 'Thank you!'

The grandfather clock replied:

'Tick-tock, tick-tock,
You spoke to each other between twelve o'clock.

Tock-tick, tock-tick,
It's going on One,
Tick-tock, tick-tock,
Well done! Well done!'

Cecile's mother came out of the kitchen and said, 'What on earth are you doing, Cecile, holding poor Jean-Pierre up to the clock like that?'

'Nothing,' said Cecile.

But it had been really something, and she felt happier than she ever had in her life before as the clock repeated:

'Tick-tock, tick-tock,
  You spoke to each other
  Between twelve o'clock.
  Tock-tick, tock-tick,
  It's going on One,
  Tick-tock, tick-tock,
  Well done! Well done!'

The day Jean-Pierre was pignapped

to
**Lori and Lonni
Leonidoff**

One Saturday afternoon, early in the month of February, when even in the South of France it can be cold and rainy, Cecile and her mother came home from school. It was in Cannes some miles from their flower farm back in the hills, overlooking the sea. There Cecile's father, Monsieur Durand, grew all kinds of flowers for the market.

Because Cecile was still only nine years old she could not go to school alone. Her mother took her on the bus every morning and called for her in the afternoons.

It was a fifteen-minute walk from the bus stop to the

farm, but neither Cecile nor her mother minded the rain and chatted happily all the way.

'Have you much homework to do over the weekend?' Madame Durand asked.

Cecile replied, 'I have arithmetic and grammar, and history and some geography, and spelling words to learn, and a drawing to make. I promise I'll get it done. But first I must look after Jean-Pierre. May I, please, Mummy?'

Jean-Pierre was Cecile's Guinea Pig. Next to her parents she loved him more than anyone or anything else in the world. She had bought him with savings out of her own pocket-money.

He was not just an ordinary Guinea Pig. In fact he was quite extraordinary. First of all, he was an Abyssinian Guinea Pig, with long, rough, black and brown hair and golden eyes. And secondly, he was slightly magic. For there had been one wonderful day when, helped by the old grandfather clock that stood in the hall, each had been able for an instant to talk to the other and understand what they were saying.

'Have you and Jean-Pierre been speaking to one another again?' Cecile's mother asked, with a little smile.

'No, but I'm sure we will sometime,' Cecile replied. Then she added, 'We really *did* understand one another, Mummy, while the clock struck that day . . .'

'Of course you did,' Madame Durand replied. What she was really thinking was whether everything would be in order at the farm. Her husband had gone to a perfume factory in Grasse on business that afternoon.

The hired man was ill. So she had simply locked up the house and left.

They entered the gate from the road and marched up the steep slope to their home. It stood on a terraced hill. There, in long rows of glass greenhouses, grew thousands upon thousands of carnations, and roses, geraniums, cyclamen, anemones, lilies and gladioli.

While her mother searched for her keys in her bag, to unlock the front door, Cecile, without even removing her school satchel, ran swiftly around to the old, stone barn at the back of the house to see how Jean-Pierre was getting on. For it was there he had his cage. From it he could look out the window and enjoy all of the interesting things that went on outside.

There was also a special secret place, down in the cellar of the house, where Cecile took him to feed and where their magical conversation had taken place. But during the day the barn was his home.

'Jean-Pierre! Jean-Pierre! I'm back,' Cecile cried as she raced into the barn. Then she stopped! And she stared! And then she screamed, 'Mummy! Mummy!'

For the door of Jean-Pierre's cage was wide open and Jean-Pierre was no longer in it.

At first Cecile could not believe her eyes. Of course he *must* be there. When she had left, the cage was closed and latched with a peg through a ring, which Jean-Pierre could not possibly get at. But now the peg hung loose on its string. The door stood open. And there was no Guinea Pig.

She ran to the house where Madame Durand had just

appeared at the back door. There was a hope, even though a faint one, that she had left Jean-Pierre in the cellar and had forgotten to put him in his cage that morning.

While her mother, startled, asked, 'Darling, whatever's the matter?' Cecile brushed past her and clattered down the cellar steps to the old arch and the ledge, their secret place. But there was no Jean-Pierre there either.

Back up the stairs, two at a time, went Cecile, to throw herself sobbing into her mother's arms.

'Mummy! Mummy! Something's happened to Jean-Pierre. He's gone!'

Her mother attempted to calm her, saying, 'Now darling, don't cry. How could he be? He couldn't have got out of his cage.'

But Cecile only cried harder. 'But he isn't there. Come and look.' Taking her by the hand, she drew her across the space to the barn. Just then, with a clatter and

a roar, the estate car with her father returned from Grasse.

He looked most astonished to see Cecile in such a state and said, 'Here, here, what's all this about? Whatever is the matter?'

'Papa! Mummy! It's Jean-Pierre, he's been pignapped,' was all that Cecile was able to say.

'Pignapped?' said Monsieur Durand in surprise. 'Surely you mean kidnapped.'

'But he was a Guinea Pig,' Cecile sobbed. 'So it must have been pignappers.'

They went into the barn, all three of them, and there

was no doubt about it. There was certainly no Abyssinian Guinea Pig in the cage and a search revealed that neither was he hidden in, behind, or under anything.

All the crying, tumult and excitement brought Bobi the dog, Coco the cat and Gris-Gris the rabbit around to investigate.

Monsieur Durand loved Cecile very much and took her unhappiness seriously. He said, 'A thief! Do you think so? Is there anything else missing?'

But a quick look around showed that this was not the case. Although, if a thief had visited the farm during their absence he would have been lucky. For instance, the weekend meat, left by the butcher's boy, was on the back steps of the house; so was a cake that Cecile's mother had ordered. Also there were some parcel-post packages delivered, including boxes of valuable flower seeds that had been sent from Aix-en-Provence. And Cecile's bicycle was still safely inside the doorway of the barn. You would think that if a burglar wanted anything it would be that, because it was still beautifully new and shiny. It had been a present for Christmas.

Cecile's father remarked, too, that none of the livestock about the courtyard looked at all nervous or acted uneasily. Bobi was an excellent watchdog. They would have been disturbed if some stranger had entered the property and tried to break into the house.

But nothing had been touched. Everything else was exactly where it had been before. Only the peg that latched the cage was dangling by its string. Jean-Pierre was undoubtedly missing and for Cecile this was quite the most terrible thing that had ever happened to her.

She went to search the farm on the possible chance that somehow Jean-Pierre might have managed to work the peg free and was wandering.

If he had been somewhere under a bush, Bobi surely would have snuffled him out as he accompanied her. Cecile had cried to him, as well as to Coco and Gris-Gris – 'Oh, Bobi, Coco and Gris-Gris – if you could only talk and tell me what has happened to Jean-Pierre. For all of you were here and must have seen whatever it was, or where he went.'

But of course they could not.

Cecile ran through all the greenhouses, one after the other, not even aware of the warm sweet smell of the potted flowers, already in bloom.

She went to all their favourite places; down by the brook, and into the glen in the woods at the top of the hill. She looked through the plum and apple orchard, where the bare branches of the trees were not yet in bud. She even went up into the attic, where she and Jean-Pierre used to spend rainy afternoons together.

It grew dark. Poor Cecile, by now using a torch and hoping that the shine might pick up the reflection from his golden eyes, was still searching and crying, 'Jean-Pierre, Jean-Pierre, where are you?' when her mother called her in to supper.

She might just as well not have come to the table, for all that she was able to eat. She just sat there with the tears streaming down her face. Her parents tried to

comfort her with different kinds of explanations. None of these made up for the fact that Jean-Pierre was still missing.

When her mother put her to bed, she held her closely and said, 'Come, my darling, you mustn't cry or worry any more. Papa has said that tomorrow we will go to the *Gendarmerie* and say that Jean-Pierre has been lost or stolen. Perhaps they will put up a notice so that if someone in the neighbourhood finds him, he will be returned.'

In France the *Gendarmerie* is a police station and the *Gendarmes* are a kind of country police.

After the light was put out and her mother left her, Cecile cried quietly for a long time before at last she fell asleep. For it was worse even than if she had come home to find that Jean-Pierre had died suddenly, from a cold on his chest, or overeating. It was the not knowing that was so awful; where he might be or what exactly had happened.

The next morning, Madame Durand kept her promise. After breakfast she packed herself and Cecile into the estate car and they drove off to the *Gendarmerie* in the village, several miles from the farm.

It began not at all encouragingly. The building was old and appeared to be half falling down. When they entered they found themselves in a whitewashed room that was quite smelly. Behind a desk sat a fierce-looking man in uniform, reading a newspaper. He did not bother to take any notice of Cecile and her mother, but let them stand there until he had finished. Then he looked up and inquired, not too pleasantly, what it was they wanted.

He was probably thoroughly put out at having to work on Sunday, for when Cecile's mother began to explain that her little girl had lost a Guinea Pig, he growled, 'And what do you expect *us* to do? If we were to bother over every cat or dog that has strayed, we'd have no time for anything else. And as for Guinea Pigs . . .' And the silence that followed showed very plainly what he thought of *them*.

But Madame Durand was not to be put off like that and said, 'You don't understand, Monsieur. This is a most unusual one, an Abyssinian, and his loss means a great deal to my daughter. We think that he might have been stolen.'

'Ha,' the *Gendarme* sneered, 'perhaps, then, you'd like to speak to the Chief Inspector?'

Of course he did not mean this at all and was only trying to be clever. For he was certain that no one would dare to trouble so high an official over the matter of the disappearance of a Guinea Pig – Abyssinian, Egyptian, French or whatever it was. All he really wished to do was to get rid of the pair.

But Cecile's mother said bravely, 'Yes, please, we *would* like to see him.'

The *Gendarme* looked surprised and said, 'Then wait here.' He arose and disappeared through a door.

The two sat upon a hard bench while they read the notices affixed to the walls, about burglars wanted and valuable articles lost. There were also long, tiresome lists of things one was not allowed to do, according to laws passed as far back as 1830.

When the *Gendarme* returned he was looking even more surprised. This time he was almost polite as he said, 'The Chief will see you. Come this way, please.'

For the first time Cecile began to take heart. They were shown into a more pleasant office that did not smell, and the Chief Inspector, at his desk, was as different from the *Gendarme* as day is from night.

His hair, which was cut short and stood up straight like a shoe brush, was turning grey. He had a red, square-shaped face from which shone a pair of friendly blue eyes. For the rest, he was short and stocky and in all made a most agreeable impression.

When Madame Durand had introduced herself he

begged them to be seated and said, 'Of course, Madame, I have heard of your farm and hope that you will ask me to visit it some day. One knows that the flowers grown there are better than any others in this area. And now, what is it I can do for you?'

Indeed, after their reception by the first *Gendarme*, Cecile was astonished at the kindness and gentleness of this high official.

What neither she nor her mother were aware of, was that the Chief Inspector had only recently arrived at this post, and was anxious to make a good impression. He was a clever man, who had learned by experience. If a policeman is on good terms with all of those whom he serves or protects, his work is made ten times easier when it comes to any kind of trouble.

Therefore he chose to treat the disappearance of the pet of this small, unhappy-looking girl, as though it had been a robbery of jewels, furs and paintings from some millionaire's villa.

'Will you describe this animal to me?' he asked, after Madame Durand had quickly told him their story.

'Oh, yes,' said Cecile at once. 'He is so big – and she placed her hands apart the exact size, for she had cuddled him so often that she knew to the smallest part of an inch – 'and so high. And his hair is long and rough and sort of black, but not a real proper black, more of a browny-black. You see, he is an Abyssinian Guinea Pig. He has a pink nose and pink feet and white whiskers. And his eyes aren't like the eyes of other

Guinea Pigs, but yellow like – like buttercups,' she ended.

'Eyes . . . yellow . . . like buttercups,' wrote the Inspector, who had been taking down everything Cecile was saying.

'Have you a photograph of this little beast?' he then asked.

Cecile's mother and Cecile were prepared for this, too, for they had often taken snapshots of Jean-Pierre in various poses. They had not forgotten to have the best of these with them.

'Aha,' said the Inspector, after examining several, 'excellent! We will have posters prepared, some in French and a number in English as well, for as you know, many British live in this neighbourhood.'

He then addressed himself to Madame Durand. 'You think, perhaps, that this valuable animal might have been stolen? Do you suspect anyone who might have come to the farm during your absence?'

'Oh no!' Madame Durand replied. 'The post was delivered; the bakery had been; the meat I ordered had arrived. The postman, the baker and the butcher's boy – we know them all well. And nothing else had been touched, you see.'

The Chief tapped his pencil on the desk reflectively and said, 'Hmmm. There have been some cat thieves about. We have had a number of complaints from people that their cats have disappeared, or been stolen.'

'Cat thieves?' queried Cecile's mother, while Cecile's

eyes opened wide with astonishment. 'Why would anyone wish to steal a cat?'

'Ho, ho, Madame!' the Chief laughed, his eyes filled with wisdom. 'You enter a restaurant. There is rabbit stew on the menu. In good faith you order. You think you're eating rabbit?'

He said, 'Ho, ho!' once more and then fell silent for an instant before continuing, 'This is a wicked world and not everyone is honest. And then there is the fur of the cat which is good for rheumatism, or if you have a cold on the chest, worn next to the body. These men steal them, sell the carcasses to the butcher and the skins to the apothecary.'

Cecile had to call upon all her courage not to disgrace herself by bursting into tears before this official, because of the horror of the pictures he had created in her mind. The thought of someone using Jean-Pierre as a chest protector was more than she could bear.

As though to deny that such a thing could happen to him, she said, 'But Jean-Pierre is magic. He can talk – at least once we spoke to one another and I could understand him and he could understand me.'

Now it came out what Cecile's mother really thought about this story, for she said, 'Come, Cecile, you mustn't be silly. We are taking up enough of this very kind Inspector's time as it is. Guinea Pigs do not talk.'

The Inspector gave Madame Durand a friendly, understanding look which said only too plainly: *Have no fear, Madame, I understand what children are like.* Aloud he remarked with a little smile, 'What a pity,

since he is so clever, that he couldn't send us a message
to say where he is and what has happened to him.'

Cecile said, 'Perhaps he will.' For she did think
Jean-Pierre clever enough for this. In her mind she

could even see him sitting down somewhere with pen
and ink and paper, writing to her.

'Well then,' said the Chief, and showed that the
interview was over by rising. 'In the meantime we will
do all that we can, and hope that this little tragedy will
come to a happy ending. I will send a man over to your
farm this afternoon, who will inspect the premises and

perhaps discover something which will aid us in our search.'

Cecile was so grateful to the Inspector that when she came to say goodbye she kissed him and received in return a fond pat. When they left she had the feeling that she had made a real friend.

The Inspector himself felt satisfied that he had done an excellent morning's work in getting to know his neighbours. And that afternoon he actually did send one of his *Gendarmes* around to the flower farm.

The *Gendarme* was a tall, thin – oh, very tall – young man with a small, black moustache and dark brown eyes. He was so tall that when he bent down to look at something through his magnifying glass, he reminded Cecile of his own jointed, measuring ruler doubled over.

He was most serious in his work and kindly disposed as well. He permitted Cecile to go about with him while he poked and probed and pried and hunted. He measured everything; Jean-Pierre's cage, the width of the door, the distance of the cage from the window. Occasionally he would look at something through the magnifying glass.

When Cecile asked what he was doing, he replied, 'Looking for clues.'

'What are clues?' Cecile asked.

'Some trace the robber leaves behind; some mistake he makes,' the *Gendarme* explained. 'Every burglar leaves some kind of mark somewhere which gives him away.'

But alas, this one apparently had been unusually clever, for nothing seemed to turn up.

The detective took a small bottle of white powder
from his pocket and a fine brush and dusted the peg that
fitted into the latch of Jean-Pierre's cage.

'What's that you're doing?' Cecile asked.

'Looking for fingerprints.'

'What are fingerprints?'

'Well,' replied the *Gendarme* with great patience,
'look at your own fingertips. See, they are all little lines

69

and loops. There's oil in your skin and whatever you touch leaves behind a tiny impression of these markings. If we catch someone, we compare the marks made by his fingers with those found on the scene of the crime. Since no two prints in the world are alike, if they match up we know that we have the criminal.'

Cecile thought this the most thrilling and exciting thing she had ever heard. But alas, when the peg had been thoroughly dusted, there was such a jumble of prints made by everybody about the place, and the surface was so small, that the detective was no wiser.

'Well, we must continue to search elsewhere,' he said, and made more notes in a little book he carried, which he had already half-filled.

For some reason he had formed an opinion that whoever had stolen or 'pignapped' Jean-Pierre might still be lurking about. So he searched the house, opening cupboards with great suddenness. But the only result was that when he did it in Cecile's room, all her toys fell out on top of him. This made Cecile laugh in spite of her misery. And the detective, who was a good sort, joined in the laughter.

It was late afternoon when he had filled his notebook and completed his investigation. He took his departure saying, 'I will make my report directly to the Chief.'

'But did you find any clues?' Cecile begged.

The *Gendarme* chose to be slightly mysterious, and replied, 'Perhaps yes, perhaps no.' The truth was that he had found none at all and was just as much in the dark as to what had happened to one browny-black, pink-footed, buttercup-eyed, Abyssinian Guinea Pig as when he had arrived.

The Chief had lost no time in keeping his promise about the posters. For the next day, on their way home from school, Cecile and her mother caught a glimpse from the bus of a small handbill affixed to a brick wall. From it stared the face of Jean-Pierre and they were able to read a few words in large type:

LOST, STRAYED OR STOLEN
REWARD

But days passed and neither the posters scattered about, nor the visit of the detective brought Jean-Pierre back. Cecile grew sadder and sadder as she thought she might never see her friend again.

It affected her marks in school. Cecile was a clever child, always near the top of her class. Now, through worry and inattention she was well down towards the bottom. She made no excuses for her bad marks, but she told all her particular friends about her sadness. Some already knew, having seen the notices advertising the loss of Jean-Pierre.

Instead of listening to what the teachers were saying, her mind was engaged with the awful pictures of what might have happened to Jean-Pierre.

She saw him turning on a spit. She imagined his skin being used upon a rheumaticky old gentleman to warm his bones. It had grown colder and the rise of hills just behind her home had a white mantle of snow. She saw poor Jean-Pierre somewhere, alone, freezing in a snowstorm.

Or he was starving – or being overfed. Or someone cruel had stolen him and was beating or teasing him. Or perhaps he had wandered off and been run over by a lorry and was somewhere on the road flattened like a pancake.

Each night Cecile placed a number of his favourite dishes in a row outside the barn, in the hope that if he were hiding anywhere he would be tempted to return. There would be a dish of lettuce, one with a carrot, another with crumbs of cake and a fourth with a bit of fruit. On the fifth there was a slice of pumpkin. There was milk, of course, and a final treat of some pomegranate seeds of which Jean-Pierre was especially fond.

But in the morning all she ever found was that mice had been at the crumbs, or perhaps snails had got into the lettuce. Once she found Coco drinking the milk.

None of the things Jean-Pierre really liked had been touched.

It was not until Thursday that Cecile awoke and was aware of something like the very special feeling she had had on that magic Sunday some months before.

To begin with, Thursday is special for children in France. On that day the schools are closed instead of on Saturday. All of the school holidays are quite different from ours.

On this particular one, Cecile felt that this was the kind of day on which something might be going to happen. And because of this she remembered the clock that had revealed the secret of when and how she and Jean-Pierre would be able to talk to one another.

It stood in the hall, in the very same place where it had been for the last two hundred years. It was very old and wise, almost as old as the house itself.

It was a grandfather clock, so tall it reached almost to the ceiling. On its dial was painted the sun and the moon. In the middle were the holes for the key to wind up the works and the striker. At the bottom there was a place for the day of the month. Cecile always thought it looked like a face, a wise and friendly one. Sometimes when she passed she felt that the clock was following her with its eyes.

Now, because of the special way she felt that morning, she got up and, padding down the stairs from her bedroom into the hall, went straight to the clock. There, she folded her hands and, looking up into its face, begged, 'Oh clock, please help me to find Jean-Pierre!'

First the clock said only, 'Tick-tock, tick-tock.'

But then it changed, as Cecile remembered it had done before and instead of saying, 'Tick-tock,' it went, 'Tock-tick, tock-tick.'

She thought that it was smiling at her and she waited, breathlessly, for what would happen next.

Then, clearly she heard the clock say:

'Tock-tick, tock-tick,
Be quick, be quick!
Be wise, be wise
Use your eyes! Use your eyes!'

And after that it said nothing more, and from its
'Tock-tick' went back to its old 'Tick-tock' and that
was all.

'Be wise, be wise,
Use your eyes! Use your eyes!'

What could it mean? The old clock had spoken in a
riddle once before, and Cecile had had to guess. Now
she tried to think very hard what it was the clock meant
her to do.

Use her eyes? But of course she used her eyes all the
time. Otherwise how would she be able to see anything?
And what had that to do with being wise? Wise, she
supposed, could mean being clever. This was easy
enough for the clock to say, but not quite so simple to
be.

But the clock had repeated twice, 'Use your eyes!
Use your eyes!' Did this mean that she was to look
twice at everything, or notice more sharply all that was
going on around her? Well, if that was the case, she
would look three times, to make sure that she missed
nothing that might help her to find Jean-Pierre.

She looked hard, long, and twice or three times at

what she saw that morning and so she noticed many things that she had never seen before.

For instance, the shell of her breakfast egg – what a marvellous thing it was! So were the veins of a leaf and the delicate velvet of a flower petal. Everything that came beneath her glance looked different. She saw the perfect colour in the red comb of the rooster, and that on the legs of the chickens were scales, like those on the body of a snake.

Even her bicycle looked different when she saw how beautifully it was made and how each part fitted into the other. And when she did her homework she became aware of the paper on which the words were printed. The pictures, she noted, were made up of thousands and thousands of little dots, light and dark.

What a new and joyful game this was, using her eyes. The farmyard looked new, the trees, the buildings, and the way the winter sun shone on the grey-blue Mediterranean sea, far below.

And there were the people, too. She saw how the back of Marcel, the farmhand, was bent from years of stooping to dig in the ground and leaning over flower-pots to tend the seedlings. When the postman came, she noticed there was a scar on his face, running from the corner of one eye to the end of his chin. She remembered hearing once that he had been wounded and very brave in the war, and had won a medal. She wondered why she had never seen the scar before.

She hoped that perhaps in the letters there would be some word from the Inspector about Jean-Pierre, but there was none. So she continued to obey the advice of the clock and look at everything twice and often three times.

Just before eleven o'clock, the butcher's boy came bicycling up the path with the meat order. It seemed to Cecile that she really saw him, too, for the very first time. For whoever remembers, or looks at, the butcher's

boy, who is never more than a white apron and a rather grubby fist handing over a parcel?

This time, Cecile was sitting on the back doorstep as he arrived. She was able to see him clearly, and thought that he was rather a poor-looking creature. He had a long, narrow face that was unfortunately full of spots, a beaked nose, and his eyes did not exactly match. His skin seemed to have no colour whatever. He had yellow, wavy hair which stood up from the front of his head like a cock's comb. His legs and arms were thin and his teeth were not very good either.

However, he whistled beautifully, and coming to a halt he dismounted, leaning his bicycle against the side of the house.

'Good morning,' he said. 'Here is the leg of lamb your mother ordered.'

At this moment the clock in the front hall struck eleven. It had a loud, booming note that could be heard all over the house.

It brought once more to Cecile's mind the rhyme it had given her:

'Be wise, be wise,
 Use your eyes! Use your eyes!'

And so she looked very hard at the butcher's boy once, twice – and the third time she thought that her heart would stand still.

For there, on the breast of his white apron, she saw three longish, browny-black hairs; one of them more brown than black, the other more black than brown, and the third all black but with brown at the tip. Instantly she felt that they could only be the hairs of Jean-Pierre and that this was the means he had taken of sending her a message to let her know where he was.

But supposing they were not? Supposing the butcher's boy owned a tortoiseshell cat? She had to make certain.

'Be wise, be wise,' the clock had advised.

'Wait,' she said, 'I'll take it in to Mummy who will see if it is all right.'

With that she took the parcel, dropped it on the kitchen table and, as fast as she could, ran downstairs into the cellar. She put on the light and went to the place where she always used to feed Jean-Pierre, and where certainly he would have left some hairs from his long, rough coat.

Sure enough, there they were on the stone ledge. Several were exactly like those she had seen on the apron of the butcher's boy.

She hurried upstairs and out to the back. But by the time she arrived, he was gone. Just passing through the gate she saw the thin, white figure and the last of the yellow, wavy mass of hair standing up from his head.

So there it was. Jean-Pierre had sent her a message to tell her where he was!

But why, or how, or for what reason he was there she could not imagine. Yet she was certain it was so, unless indeed the butcher's boy *should* own a tortoise-shell cat with exactly the same colour hair.

But if this was so, why would the clock have spoken

to her this morning? Why would the day have felt so special? Pleased as she was at the sign that perhaps, after all, Jean-Pierre was safe and well, there was still a great mystery about the whole business.

For it never dawned upon Cecile that the butcher's boy might have stolen Jean-Pierre. Why should he do such a thing? After all, he had been delivering meat to their house as long as she could remember and never had anything disappeared. Cecile had quite a different picture of a thief in her mind. A burglar was a big, ugly man with a mask over his eyes, a torch in one hand, a sack in the other.

She wondered whether she ought to tell her father and mother, but decided not to do so.

But she did know what she *would* do, for when her homework was done, she had permission to take her bicycle and ride around the country lanes, as far as the village.

As soon as lunch was over she rode away. Twenty minutes later, she was sitting in the same, smelly room in the *Gendarmerie*, looking at the same notices on the same dirty whitewashed walls, waiting to see the Chief Inspector.

When at last she was admitted to his office, he arose and greeted her as politely as though her mother had been there too. He offered a chair and then, seating himself, sighed and said, 'Alas, Mademoiselle, our attempts have been all in vain. No one has reported so much as a sight of your Guinea Pig, and my detective has not been able to discover how the animal escaped.'

Cecile said, 'Thank you very much. But that is why I have come to see you. I know where Jean-Pierre is.'

'Eh? What's that you say?' the Inspector asked, full of interest. 'You've found him? He's back?'

Cecile replied, 'No! But I know where he is. He's with the butcher's boy.'

'The butcher's boy!' The Inspector could not keep the astonishment out of his voice. 'How do you know?'

It was on the tip of Cecile's tongue to tell him about the three hairs on the apron. They might indeed be what the detective had called a clue. On the other hand, supposing the butcher's boy really did have a tortoise-shell cat, or even a dog with a rough brown-black coat? It was one thing to be certain of something when she was at home and safe. But it was quite another to find herself alone in the police station, even though the Inspector was so kind and patient.

And so instead of mentioning the hairs, she simply said, 'Jean-Pierre sent me a message.'

'Oh, did he, indeed? And what did he write?'

Cecile had to think how to reply. 'It wasn't *that* kind of a message, really. It was a different sort of a one, just to let me know that he was alive and with the butcher's boy.'

'But why with him, Mademoiselle?'

'Because,' said Cecile, 'that's where Jean-Pierre's message said he was.'

The Inspector sighed and asked, 'What is the name of your mother's butcher?'

'It's Monsieur Carossi.'

The Inspector nodded and noted down the name. Then, leaning forward on his desk with his hands folded, he said earnestly, but most kindly, 'Dear Mademoiselle Cecile, I understand very well that sometimes things can happen in the world of children which cannot take place in that of the grown-ups. But if I were to arrest the butcher's boy and the Judge were to ask me, "Why have you brought this poor, young man before me?" what am I to reply? That Mademoiselle Cecile Durand received a message from her Guinea Pig that this young man had stolen him? We should all look very foolish indeed, would we not? Also, one of the most wicked of all things is to accuse someone falsely.'

Cecile saw that this was so and that there was nothing more to be said. The Inspector did not believe at all that Jean-Pierre had sent her a message. She now felt, also, that if she had told him about the three hairs on the apron, he would have considered her even more silly.

'But we will keep an eye open,' the Inspector ended.

Cecile thanked him politely, made her little bob when she shook hands to say goodbye and went out, got on her bicycle and rode home.

The Inspector remained at his desk for a moment, thinking of the strange ways of children and the things they imagined they heard, or saw.

Because he was a clever policeman, he already knew all about Carossi, the butcher. He sold good, clean meat and gave honest weight. And he knew about the butcher's boy, too, whose name was Armand Allard. He was seventeen years old and had gone to work for the butcher at the age of fourteen, to help his widowed mother. She herself earned money by going to other people's houses to clean by the hour.

The Inspector even knew where the butcher's boy lived. It was behind his own house, in a small cottage down the lane. For it so happened that twice a week Madame Allard came to help out his wife with the scrubbing and polishing.

Whatever had led this child to the belief that somehow this hardworking boy had her Guinea Pig, the chief wondered?

At this moment the telephone rang. It was important business and the Inspector put the whole affair of Cecile, Jean-Pierre and the butcher's boy out of his mind.

As for Cecile, it was all too much for her and when she arrived home she did not know what to do.

When her mother called to her, 'Did you have a nice ride, darling?' she was tempted to tell her where she had been, and why she had gone. But then she remembered that during their first visit to the office of the Inspector her mother had laughed at the idea that she and Jean-Pierre had ever understood one another. In front of him had told her not to be silly. And so she could bring herself to say no more than, 'Yes, Mummy, thank you.'

She went and sat down upon the cellar steps with her head in her hands.

All kinds of thoughts and pictures passed through her mind. One of them was of herself and the Inspector pouncing upon the butcher's boy and accusing him of having stolen Jean-Pierre. Then they found that the hairs on his apron exactly matched those of a large Airedale dog that was frisking about.

Oh no! It was impossible to think of trying to find out where the butcher's boy lived and go there, or even to ask him the next time he came.

But then, if there was no truth in Jean-Pierre's message, why had the day begun with that magic feeling? And, above all, why had the grandfather clock spoken to her as it had once before upon another magic day, with its rhyming riddle?

Cecile arose and ran up the steps quickly to see whether the clock might have anything further to say to her. But this time there was no change in the steady 'tick-tock, tick-tock, tick-tock'.

Yet, just as she was about to turn away, she caught the face smiling at her, as though it knew something. Or, at least, she thought she did.

It seemed to say, 'Have courage, Cecile. The day is not over. The magic is not yet finished. Many things can still happen.'

And at that the old clock shivered. Then it shook. Then it buzzed. Then it whirred and its insides made the noise like someone falling downstairs, before it finally struck six.

Cecile thought that there was not very much of the day left for things to happen, and wished they would begin.

At supper time she was so unusually quiet that her father asked her if she felt ill, for he was used to having her chattering away.

But it was only because she was concentrating so hard upon whatever might come, so that she would be prepared for it.

When supper was over and they were all in the sitting-room, Monsieur Durand read his papers. His wife worked at her needlepoint. Cecile looked over her history work and geography lessons for tomorrow's school.

But she found it very hard to keep her mind upon the names of the kings of France, or where the River Loire was to be found. She was longing to hold Jean-Pierre in her arms once more and wondering whether she would indeed ever see him again, now that this magic day was drawing to its close.

With dismay and a sinking of her heart, she heard the old clock in the hall go through all the noises it had to make before it could strike. Then she listened to the deep, booming notes of eight o'clock.

She hoped against hope that perhaps this time her mother would not notice. But no. At the very last stroke, Madame Durand laid down her needlework and said, 'Bedtime, Cecile.'

And so it was over. This was final, the end of the day. Sadly, Cecile closed her books, arose, kissed her father good night and started for the stairs. Her mother would be coming up to her later.

She had placed her foot only upon the first step, when

there was a most astonishing glare that passed across the windows of the sitting-room, almost as though lightning had flashed. This was followed by the sound of a car arriving, which caused Monsieur Durand to say, 'Now, whoever can that be, coming here at this hour?' In the courtyard Bobi set up a tremendous barking.

Cecile remained still. Could this possibly be it?

Footsteps were heard outside. The doorbell rang and Monsieur Durand went to see who it was.

Quickly, before anyone could say anything to her, Cecile nipped back into the sitting-room. She heard her father at the door say, 'Oh, good evening, Inspector. But of course, of course! Come in.'

Then there entered the Inspector and a weeping woman with a black shawl over her head. They were followed by the butcher's boy, so white and pale that his spots stood out more than ever. His formerly gay cock's comb of yellow hair now fell limply over his eyes.

And in his arms was Jean-Pierre!

Cecile was so thrilled and excited that she could neither move nor speak.

'So,' began the Inspector, 'I have but two questions to ask. Madame Durand, is this the boy who delivers your meat?'

'Yes,' replied Cecile's mother, 'it is.'

'Very well, then. Mademoiselle Cecile, is this your Guinea Pig?'

At last Cecile found that she could speak and cried, 'Oh, yes, yes! That's my Jean-Pierre.'

In a voice of thunder and pointing to the butcher's

boy, whose limbs had begun to shake most alarmingly, he said, 'Restore the animal to this young lady, at once!'

Trembling and perspiring the youth handed the Guinea Pig to Cecile, who took him with a cry of joy, 'Oh, Jean-Pierre! My Jean-Pierre!' She kissed and cuddled him. Jean-Pierre squeaked with pleasure and then sneezed six times in a row, out of sheer happiness at being returned to his mistress.

But the affair was not yet ended.

For the Inspector was speaking again. He said, 'I am astounded! I am shocked that such a miserable event should take place in my district!'

The legs of Armand, the butcher's boy, were now shaking even more. The woman with the shawl, who was his mother, let large tears drop from her eyes as the Chief continued.

'Tonight, after supper, I decided to go for a little stroll. Somehow I found my footsteps turning in the direction of the lane where Madame Allard and her son live. I had upon my mind the story Mademoiselle here had told me this afternoon, about receiving a message from her Guinea Pig.'

Madame Durand looked at Cecile in surprise.

'Absurd, of course,' he continued, 'but then with children one really never knows. I decided to pay a visit to Madame Allard, to hand her some wages, and while I was there I heard a strange squeaking and then a disturbance from the back of the cottage.

'And there,' and he paused for the impression he was about to make, 'and there, what do you suppose I found?' He pointed to the quaking boy, 'This idiot, with the little Guinea Pig in an old parrot cage, trying to feed it a pork chop! Imagine! A pork chop for a herbivore!'

Cecile had not the faintest idea what a herbivore was, but only knew that Jean-Pierre had not been fed properly during his absence.

'Oh, poor Jean-Pierre!' she cried and held him away from her to inspect him more carefully. She could see that he had lost some weight, but otherwise appeared to be in perfect health and spirits.

'And so, villain,' thundered the Inspector, 'you are now a thief! And do you know what happens to a thief? He is sentenced to jail and is locked up in a cell and fed on bread and water!'

At this Madame Allard fell upon her knees and raising her folded hands cried, 'Mercy, mercy, gentlemen and ladies! The boy is the only support of my old age. He is a good boy. He didn't mean to do it. Oh, be merciful to a poor widow!'

Armand, in the meantime, was looking more miserable than anyone Cecile had seen in her whole life. His lips were trembling. The sweat was rolling from his brow and his eyes were more crossed than ever.

Cecile felt sorry for the mother, but not quite so much for the butcher's boy. It was wrong of him to steal her Guinea Pig.

'Scoundrel!' the Inspector addressed the terrified Armand. 'Why did you do this? Speak, if you have anything to say!'

The effort was almost too much for the unhappy, frightened lad. Yet somehow he managed to bring out the words, 'Because he was so beautiful. I loved him. I couldn't help myself.'

And suddenly Cecile felt her heart melt at these words. In the twinkling of an eye everything seemed different from what it had been before. The butcher's boy, too, loved Jean-Pierre and had wanted him, as she had the first time she had seen him in the window of the pet shop. It was not his fault that he was stupid and had tried to feed Jean-Pierre on pork chops. What else would a butcher's boy be able to think of, except meat? And if she had felt sorry for the mother before, she now felt ten times more sorry for Armand.

Almost before she knew what was happening, she heard herself say, 'But he didn't really steal Jean-Pierre. He only borrowed him. I told him he could do so some day.'

Now it was the turn of Cecile's father to become angry. He cried, 'What? You gave him permission to borrow the wretched beast? You put us all at sixes and sevens going to the police station and making complaints to the Inspector, and had this poor fellow dragged here at night and threatened with jail and bread and water? Why didn't you tell us this before?'

'I forgot,' Cecile replied, simply.

It wasn't exactly true, of course. But it was what is known as a white lie, which is sometimes told to help someone. And now that she knew that it was all because the butcher's boy, too, had loved Jean-Pierre, she could not bear to see him punished.

Besides which, it was clear to her now that Armand had cuddled him, giving the clever, clever, little Guinea Pig the opportunity to leave three of his hairs on the apron and thus send his message to Cecile.

Surprisingly, it was the Inspector who suddenly lost his thunder and proved to be not at all angry at what Cecile had just revealed.

'Oh, well,' he said, 'children do forget such things sometimes. We mustn't be too hard on them. And now that we know that Armand only borrowed the Guinea Pig and was intending to bring him back, there is, of course, no charge against him and we can go home.'

For, being the kind man he was, even though he had been making a fuss, he had not at all liked the idea of putting the poor boy into prison.

Madame Allard rose to her feet, 'God will bless you for this,' she said.

Madame Durand went to Cecile and took her in her arms and squeezed her hard, for she understood and was pleased with what Cecile had done for the unfortunate boy.

Only Cecile's father looked somewhat bewildered at the turn events had taken.

'There is only one question I would be grateful to have answered,' the Inspector said. 'How did our little Mademoiselle here know where Jean-Pierre was, even after she – ahem,' and here he coughed, '"forgot" that she had given Armand permission to borrow him?'

Now Cecile was greatly tempted to say about the three hairs she had seen.

But she only said once more, 'It was Jean-Pierre. I told you. He sent me a message.'

The Inspector shrugged, then sighed, and finally bade them good night and all three left.

As they passed before the window for a moment on the way to the car, they were outlined by the light of the moon. It was seen that the Inspector had Armand Allard by the ear and was giving it a good twisting. Cecile's father wondered why he was doing this, if the lad were innocent.

And that was the end of the story of the pignapping and the secret clue of the three, black-browny hairs about which only Cecile and Jean-Pierre knew.

Only one more thing.

When Cecile asked, 'Mummy, please may Jean-Pierre sleep in my room with me tonight?' her mother replied, 'Yes, of course. But only this once.'

And when Madame Durand, a little later on, went upstairs for a goodnight kiss and tuck in, she found that

Jean-Pierre had been put to bed in the little wicker cradle of Cecile's favourite doll, who had been turned out and was lying face-down on the rug. The Guinea Pig was fast asleep.

Some more stories

Ursula Moray Williams
The Three Toymakers (illustrated) 35p

When the king offers a thousand gold pieces for the best toy,
all the villagers of Drüssl are sure that old Peter Toymaker
or his adopted son Rudi will win, but they don't know
about crafty old Malkin's unusual and very angelic-seeming
doll, who is not as innocent as she looks . . .

The Toymaker's Daughter (illustrated) 35p

The adventure begins when Danny and Niclo find the
eight-year-old daughter of Malkin the Toymaker on the
mountain-side. It is all very strange, and old Malkin learns
that happiness isn't something you can carve out of wood.

Malkin's Mountain (illustrated) 35p

This time, wicked old Malkin, jealous of the toymakers of
Drüssl, decides to move the mountain and steal all its pine
trees for himself and his new toymaking business! But he
doesn't get away with it because Rudi Toymaker, his doll-
queen and his wooden soldiers set out to defeat him.